Ralph Abercrombie:

SALLY BOWLES

By Christopher Isherwood

SALLY BOWLES

Christopher Isherwood

PUBLISHED BY LEONARD AND VIRGINIA WOOLF AT THE
HOGARTH PRESS, 52 TAVISTOCK SQUARE, LONDON, W.C.2
1937

First published 1937

MADE AND PRINTED IN GREAT BRITAIN BY THE
GARDEN CITY PRESS LTD., AT LETCHWORTH,
HERTFORDSHIRE

To
JOHN LEHMANN

SALLY BOWLES

One afternoon, early in October, I was invited to black coffee at Fritz Wendel's flat. Fritz always invited you to " black coffee," with emphasis on the black. He was very proud of his coffee. People used to say that it was the strongest in Berlin.

Fritz himself was dressed in his usual coffee-party costume—a thick white yachting sweater and very light blue flannel trousers. He greeted me with his full-lipped, luscious smile:

" 'lo, Chris! "

" Hullo, Fritz. How are you ? "

" Fine." He bent over the coffee-machine, his sleek black hair unplastering itself from his scalp and falling

7

in richly scented locks over his eyes. "This darn thing doesn't go," he added.

"How's business?" I asked.

"Lousy and terrible." Fritz grinned richly. "Or I pull off a new deal in the next month or I go as a gigolo."

"*Either* ... or ...," I corrected, from force of professional habit.

"I'm speaking a lousy English just now," drawled Fritz, with great self-satisfaction. "Sally says maybe she'll give me a few lessons."

"Who's Sally?"

"Why, I forgot. You don't know Sally. Too bad of me. Eventually she's coming around here this afternoon."

"Is she nice?"

Fritz rolled his naughty black eyes, handing me a rum-moistened cigarette from his patent tin:

" *Mar*-vellous! " he drawled. " Eventually I believe I'm getting crazy about her."

" And who is she ? What does she do ? "

" She's an English girl, an actress: sings at the Lady Windermere—hot stuff, believe me! "

" That doesn't sound much like an English girl, I must say."

" Eventually she's got a bit of French in her. Her mother was French."

A few minutes later, Sally herself arrived.

" Am I terribly late, Fritz darling ? "

" Only half of an hour, I suppose," Fritz drawled, beaming with proprietary pleasure. " May I introduce Mr. Isherwood—Miss Bowles ? Mr. Isherwood is commonly known as Chris."

" I'm not," I said. " Fritz is about

the only person who's ever called me Chris in my life."

Sally laughed. She was dressed in black silk, with a small cape over her shoulders and a little cap like a page-boy's stuck jauntily on one side of her head:

" Do you mind if I use your telephone, sweet ? "

" Sure. Go right ahead." Fritz caught my eye. " Come into the other room, Chris. I want to show you something." He was evidently longing to hear my first impressions of Sally, his new acquisition.

" For heaven's sake, don't leave me alone with this man ! " she exclaimed. " Or he'll seduce me down the telephone. He's most terribly passionate."

As she dialled the number, I noticed that her finger-nails were painted emerald green, a colour unfortunately chosen, for it called attention to her hands, which were much stained by cigarette-smoking and as dirty as a little girl's. She was dark enough to be Fritz's sister. Her face was long and thin, powdered dead white. She had very large brown eyes which should have been darker, to match her hair and the pencil she used for her eyebrows.

"Hilloo," she cooed, pursing her brilliant cherry lips as though she were going to kiss the mouthpiece: "Ist dass Du, mein Liebling?" Her mouth opened in a fatuously sweet smile. Fritz and I sat watching her, like a performance at the theatre. "Was wollen wir machen, Morgen Abend? Oh, wie wunderbar. . . . Nein, nein, ich werde bleiben Heute Abend zu Hause. Ja, ja, ich werde wirklich bleiben zu Hause.

... Auf Wiedersehen, mein Liebling
. . ."

She hung up the receiver and turned
to us triumphantly:

"That's the man I slept with last
night," she announced. "He makes
love marvellously. He's an absolute
genius at business and he's terribly
rich——" She came and sat down on
the sofa beside Fritz, sinking back into
the cushions with a sigh: "Give me
some coffee, will you, darling? I'm
simply dying of thirst."

And soon we were on to Fritz's
favourite topic: he pronounced it
Larv.

"On the average," he told us, "I'm
having a big affair every two years."

"And how long is it since you had
your last?" Sally asked.

"Exactly one year and eleven

months!" Fritz gave her his naughtiest glance.

"How marvellous!" Sally puckered up her nose and laughed a silvery little stage-laugh: "*Doo* tell me—what was the last one like?"

This, of course, started Fritz off on a complete autobiography. We had the story of his seduction in Paris, details of a holiday flirtation at Las Palmas, the four chief New York romances, a disappointment in Chicago and a conquest in Boston; then back to Paris for a little recreation, a very beautiful episode in Vienna, to London to be consoled and, finally, Berlin.

"You know, Fritz darling," said Sally, puckering up her nose at me, "*I* believe the trouble with you is that you've never really found the right woman."

" Maybe that's true——" Fritz took this idea very seriously. His black eyes became liquid and sentimental: " Maybe I'm still looking for my ideal. . . ."

" But you'll find her one day, I'm absolutely certain you will." Sally included me, with a glance, in the game of laughing at Fritz.

" You think so ? " Fritz grinned lusciously, sparkling at her.

" Don't *you* think so ? " Sally appealed to me.

" I'm sure I don't know," I said. " Because I've never been able to discover what Fritz's ideal is."

For some reason, this seemed to please Fritz. He took it as a kind of testimonial: " And Chris knows me pretty well," he chimed in. " If Chris doesn't know, well, I guess no one does."

Then it was time for Sally to go.

" I'm supposed to meet a man at the Adlon at five," she explained. " And it's six already! Never mind, it'll do the old swine good to wait. He wants me to be his mistress, but I've told him I'm damned if I will till he's paid all my debts. Why are men always such beasts ? " Opening her bag, she rapidly retouched her lips and eyebrows: " Oh, by the way, Fritz darling, could you be a perfect angel and lend me ten marks ? I haven't got a bean for a taxi."

" Why sure! " Fritz put his hand into his pocket and paid up without hesitation, like a hero.

Sally turned to me: " I say, will you come and have tea with me sometime ? Give me your telephone number. I'll ring you up."

I suppose, I thought, she imagines I've got cash. Well, this will be a lesson to her, once for all. I wrote my number in her tiny leather book. Fritz saw her out.

"Well!" he came bounding back into the room and gleefully shut the door: "What do you think of her, Chris? Didn't I tell you she was a good-looker?"

"You did indeed!"

"I'm getting crazier about her each time I see her!" With a sigh of pleasure, he helped himself to a cigarette: "More coffee, Chris?"

"No, thank you very much."

"You know, Chris, I think she took a fancy to you, too!"

"Oh, rot!"

"Honestly, I do!" Fritz seemed pleased. "Eventually I guess we'll be seeing a lot of her from now on!"

When I got back to Frl Schroeder's, I

felt so giddy that I had to lie down for half an hour on my bed. Fritz's black coffee was as poisonous as ever.

.   .   .   .

A few days later, he took me to hear Sally sing.

The Lady Windermere (which now, I hear, no longer exists) was an arty " informal " bar, just off the Tauentzien-strasse, which the proprietor had evidently tried to make look as much as possible like Montparnasse. The walls were covered with sketches on menu-cards, caricatures and signed theatrical photographs—(" To the one and only Lady Windermere." " To Johnny, with all my heart.") The Fan itself, four times life size, was displayed above the bar. There was a big piano on a platform in the middle of the room.

B   17

I was curious to see how Sally would behave. I had imagined her, for some reason, rather nervous; but she wasn't, in the least. She had a surprisingly deep husky voice. She sang badly, without any expression, her hands hanging down at her sides—yet her performance was, in its own way, effective because of her startling appearance and her air of not caring a curse what people thought of her. Her arms hanging carelessly limp, and a take-it-or-leave-it grin on her face, she sang:

> "Now I know why Mother
> Told me to be true;
> She meant me for Someone
> Exactly like you."

There was quite a lot of applause. The pianist, a handsome young man with blonde wavy hair, stood up and solemnly kissed Sally's hand. Then she sang two more songs, one in French and the other in German. These weren't so well received.

After the singing, there was a good deal more hand-kissing and a general movement towards the bar. Sally seemed to know everybody in the place. She called them all Thou and Darling. For a would-be demi-mondaine, she seemed to have surprisingly little business sense or tact. She wasted a lot of time making advances to an elderly gentleman who would obviously have preferred a chat with the barman. Later, we all got rather drunk. Then Sally had to go off to an appointment, and the manager came and sat at our table. He and Fritz talked English peerage. Fritz was in his element. I decided, as so often before, never to visit a place of this sort again.

.   .   .

Then Sally rang up, as she had promised, to invite me to tea.

She lived a long way down the Kurfürstendamm, on the last dreary stretch which rises to Halensee. I was shown into a big gloomy half-furnished room by a fat untidy landlady with a pouchy sagging jowl like a toad. There was a broken-down sofa in one corner and a faded picture of an eighteenth-century battle, with the wounded reclining on their elbows in graceful attitudes, admiring the prancings of Frederick the Great's horse.

" Oh, hullo, Chris darling! " cried Sally from the doorway. " How sweet of you to come! I was feeling most terribly lonely. I've been crying on Frau Karpf's chest. Nicht wahr, Frau Karpf ? " She appealed to the toad landlady, " ich habe geweint auf Dein

Brust." Frau Karpf shook her bosom in a toad-like chuckle.

"Would you rather have coffee, Chris, or tea?" Sally continued. "You can have either. Only I don't recommend the tea much. I don't know what Frau Karpf does to it; I think she empties all the kitchen slops together into a jug and boils them up with the tea-leaves."

"I'll have coffee, then."

"Frau Karpf, Liebling, willst Du sein ein Engel und bring zwei Tassen von Kaffee?" Sally's German was not merely incorrect; it was all her own. She pronounced every word in a mincing, specially "foreign" manner. You could tell that she was speaking a foreign language from her expression alone. "Chris darling, will you be an angel and draw the curtains?"

21

I did so, although it was still quite light outside. Sally, meanwhile, had switched on the table-lamp. As I turned from the window, she curled herself up delicately on the sofa like a cat, and, opening her bag, felt for a cigarette. But hardly was the pose complete before she'd jumped to her feet again:

"Would you like a Prairie Oyster?" She produced glasses, eggs and a bottle of Worcester sauce from the boot-cupboard under the dismantled washstand: "I practically live on them." Dexterously, she broke the eggs into the glasses, added the sauce and stirred up the mixture with the end of a fountain-pen: "They're about all I can afford." She was back on the sofa again, daintily curled up.

She was wearing the same black dress to-day, but without the cape. Instead, she had a little white collar and white cuffs. They produced a kind of theatrically chaste effect, like a nun in grand opera. "What are you laughing at, Chris?" she asked.

"I don't know," I said. But still I couldn't stop grinning. There was, at that moment, something so extraordinarily comic in Sally's appearance. She was really beautiful, with her little dark head, big eyes and finely arched nose— and so absurdly conscious of all these features. There she lay, as complacently feminine as a turtle-dove, with her poised self-conscious head and daintily arranged hands.

"Chris, you swine, do tell me why you're laughing?"

"I really haven't the faintest idea."

At this, she began to laugh, too: "You are mad, you know!"

" Have you been here long ? " I asked, looking round the large gloomy room.

" Ever since I arrived in Berlin. Let's see—that was about two months ago."

I asked what had made her decide to come out to Germany at all. Had she come alone ? No, she'd come with a girl friend. An actress. Older than Sally. The girl had been to Berlin before. She'd told Sally that they'd certainly be able to get work with the Ufa. So Sally borrowed ten pounds from a nice old gentleman and joined her.

She hadn't told her parents anything about it until the two of them had actually arrived in Germany: " I wish you'd met Diana. She was the most marvellous gold-digger you can imagine.

She'd get hold of men anywhere—it didn't matter whether she could speak their language or not. She made me nearly die of laughing. I absolutely adored her."

But when they'd been together in Berlin three weeks and no job had appeared, Diana had got hold of a banker, who'd taken her off with him to Paris.

" And left you here alone ? I must say I think that was pretty rotten of her."

" Oh, I don't know. . . . Everyone's got to look after themselves. I expect, in her place, I'd have done the same."

" I bet you wouldn't ! "

" Anyhow, I'm all right. I can always get along alone."

" How old are you, Sally ? "

" Nineteen."

" Good God! And I thought you were about twenty-five! "

" I know. Everyone does."

Frau Karpf came shuffling in with two cups of coffee on a tarnished metal tray.

" Oh, Frau Karpf, Liebling, wie wunderbar von Dich! "

" Whatever makes you stay in this house ? " I asked, when the landlady had gone out: " I'm sure you could get a much nicer room than this."

" Yes. I know I could."

" Well then, why don't you ? "

" Oh, I don't know. I'm lazy, I suppose."

" What do you have to pay here ? "

" Eighty marks a month."

" With breakfast included ? "

" No—I don't think so."

" You don't *think* so ? " I exclaimed

severely. " But surely you must know for certain ? "

Sally took this meekly: " Yes, it's stupid of me, I suppose. But, you see, I just give the old girl money when I've got some. So it's rather difficult to reckon it all up exactly."

" But, good heavens, Sally—I only pay fifty a month for my room, with breakfast, and it's ever so much nicer than this one! "

Sally nodded, but continued apologetically: " And another thing is, you see, Christopher darling, I don't quite know what Frau Karpf would do if I were to leave her. I'm sure she'd never get another lodger. Nobody else would be able to stand her face and her smell and everything. As it is, she owes three months' rent. They'd turn her out at once if they knew she hadn't any lodgers: and if they do that, she says she'll commit suicide."

" All the same, I don't see why you should sacrifice yourself for her."

" I'm not sacrificing myself, really. I quite like being here, you know. Frau Karpf and I understand each other. She's more or less what I'll be in thirty years' time. A respectable sort of land-lady would probably turn me out after a week."

" My landlady wouldn't turn you out."

Sally smiled vaguely, screwing up her nose: " How do you like the coffee, Chris darling ? "

" I prefer it to Fritz's," I said evasively.

Sally laughed: " Isn't Fritz marvel-lous ? I adore him. I adore the way he says, ' I give a damn.' "

" ' Hell, I give a damn.' " I tried to imitate Fritz. We both laughed. Sally lit another cigarette: she smoked the whole time. I noticed how old her hands looked in the lamplight. They were nervous, veined and very thin—the hands of a middle-aged woman. The green finger-nails seemed not to belong to them at all; to have settled on them by chance—like hard, bright, ugly little beetles. " It's a funny thing," she added meditatively, " Fritz and I have never slept together, you know." She paused, asked with interest: " Did you think we had ? "

" Well, yes—I suppose I did."

" We haven't. Not once . . ." she yawned. " And now I don't suppose we ever shall."

We smoked for some minutes in silence. Then Sally began to tell me

about her family. She was the daughter
of a Lancashire mill-owner. Her mother
was a Miss Bowles, an heiress with an
estate, and so, when she and Mr.
Jackson were married, they joined their
names together: " Daddy's a terrible
snob, although he pretends not to be.
My real name's Jackson-Bowles; but,
of course, I can't possibly call myself
that on the stage. People would think I
was crazy."

" I thought Fritz told me your
mother was French ? "

" No, of course not! " Sally seemed
quite annoyed. " Fritz is an idiot. He's
always inventing things."

Sally had one sister, named Betty.
" She's an absolute angel. I adore her.
She's seventeen, but she's still most
terribly innocent. Mummy's bringing
her up to be very county. Betty would

nearly die if she knew what an old whore I am. She knows absolutely nothing whatever about men."

" But why aren't you county, too, Sally ? "

" I don't know. I suppose that's Daddy's side of the family coming out. You'd love Daddy. He doesn't care a damn for anyone. He's the most marvellous business man. And about once a month he gets absolutely dead tight and horrifies all Mummy's smart friends. It was he who said I could go to London and learn acting."

" You must have left school very young ? "

" Yes. I couldn't bear school. I got myself expelled."

" However did you do that ? "

" I told the headmistress I was going to have a baby."

31

" Oh, rot, Sally, you didn't! "

" I did, honestly! There was the most terrible commotion. They got a doctor to examine me, and sent for my parents. When they found out there was nothing the matter, they were most frightfully disappointed. The headmistress said that a girl who could even think of anything so disgusting couldn't possibly be allowed to stay on and corrupt the other girls. So I got my own way. And then I pestered Daddy till he said I might go to London."

Sally had settled down in London, at a hostel, with other girl students. There, in spite of supervision, she had managed to spend large portions of the night at young men's flats: " The first man who seduced me had no idea I was a virgin until I told him afterwards. He was marvellous. I adored him. He was

32

an absolute genius at comedy parts. He's sure to be terribly famous, one day."

After a time, Sally had got crowd-work in films, and finally a small part in a touring company. Then she had met Diana.

"And how much longer shall you stay in Berlin?" I asked.

"Heaven knows. This job at the Lady Windermere only lasts another week. I got it through a man I met at the Eden Bar. But he's gone off to Vienna now. I must ring up the Ufa people again, I suppose. And then there's an awful old Jew who takes me out sometimes. He's always promising to get me a contract; but he only wants to sleep with me, the old swine. I think the men in this country are awful. They've none of them got any money,

c   33

and they expect you to let them seduce you if they give you a box of chocolates."

" How on earth are you going to manage when this job comes to an end ? "

" Oh well, I get a small allowance from home, you know. Not that that'll last much longer. Mummy's already threatened to stop it if I don't come back to England soon. . . . Of course, they think I'm here with a girl friend. If Mummy knew I was on my own, she'd simply pass right out. Anyhow, I'll get enough to support myself somehow, soon. I loathe taking money from them. Daddy's business is in a frightfully bad way now, from the slump."

" I say, Sally—if you ever really get into a mess I wish you'd let me know."

Sally laughed: " That's terribly sweet

of you, Chris. But I don't sponge on my friends."

" Isn't Fritz your friend ? " It had jumped out of my mouth. But Sally didn't seem to mind a bit.

" Oh yes, I'm awfully fond of Fritz, of course. But he's got pots of cash. Somehow, when people have cash, you feel differently about them—I don't know why."

" And how do you know I haven't got pots of cash, too ? "

" You ? " Sally burst out laughing. " Why, I knew you were hard-up the first moment I set eyes on you! "

.   .   .

The afternoon Sally came to tea with me, Frl Schroeder was beside herself with excitement. She had put on her best dress for the occasion and waved her hair. When the door-bell rang, she threw open the door with a flourish: " Herr Issyvoo," she announced, winking knowingly at me and speaking very loud, " there's a lady to see you! "

I then formally introduced Sally and Frl Schroeder to each other. Frl Schroeder was overflowing with politeness: she addressed Sally repeatedly as " Gnädiges Fräulein." Sally, with her page-boy cap stuck over one ear, laughed her silvery laugh and sat down elegantly on the sofa. Frl Schroeder hovered about her in unfeigned admiration and amazement. She had evidently never seen anyone like Sally before. When she brought in the tea there were, in place of the usual little chunks of pale unappetizing pastry, a plateful of jam tarts arranged in the shape of a star. I noticed also that Frl Schroeder had

provided us with two tiny paper serviettes, perforated at the edges to resemble
lace. (When, later, I complimented her
on these preparations, she told me that
she had always used the serviettes when
the Herr Rittmeister had had his fiancée
to tea. " Oh, yes, Herr Issyvoo. You
can depend on me! I know what
pleases a young lady! ")

" Do you mind if I lie down on your
sofa, darling ? " Sally asked, as soon as
we were alone.

" No, of course not."

Sally pulled off her cap, swung her
little velvet shoes up on to the sofa,
opened her bag and began powdering:
" I'm most terribly tired. I didn't sleep
a wink last night. I've got a marvellous
new lover."

I began to pour out the tea. Sally
gave me a sidelong glance :

" Do I shock you when I talk like that, Christopher darling ? "

" Not in the least."

" But you don't like it ? "

" It's no business of mine." I handed her the tea-glass.

" Oh, for God's sake," cried Sally, " don't start being English! Of course it's your business what you think! "

" Well then, if you want to know, it rather bores me."

This annoyed her even more than I had intended. Her tone changed: she said coldly: " I thought you'd understand." She sighed: " But I forgot—you're a man."

" I'm sorry, Sally. I can't help being a man, of course. . . . But please don't be angry with me. I only meant that when you talk like that it's really just nervousness. You're naturally rather shy with strangers, I think: so you've got into this trick of trying to bounce them into approving or disapproving of you, violently. I know, because I try it myself, sometimes. . . . Only I wish you wouldn't try it on me, because it just doesn't work and it only makes me feel embarrassed. If you go to bed with every single man in Berlin and come and tell me about it each time, you still won't convince me that you're *La Dame aux Camélias*—because, really and truly, you know, you aren't."

"No . . . I suppose I'm not——" Sally's voice was carefully impersonal. She was beginning to enjoy this conversation. I had succeeded in flattering her in some new way: " Then what *am* I, exactly, Christopher darling ? "

" You're the daughter of Mr. and Mrs. Jackson-Bowles."

Sally sipped her tea: " Yes . . . I think I see what you mean. . . . Perhaps you're right. . . . Then you think I ought to give up having lovers altogether ? "

" Certainly I don't. As long as you're sure you're really enjoying yourself."

" Of course," said Sally gravely, after a pause, " I'd never let love interfere with my work. Work comes before everything. . . . But I don't believe that a woman can be a great actress who hasn't had any love-affairs——" she broke off suddenly: " What are you laughing at, Chris ? "

" I'm not laughing."

" You're always laughing at me. Do you think I'm the most ghastly idiot ? "

" No, Sally. I don't think you're an idiot at all. It's quite true, I *was* laughing. People I like often make me want to laugh at them. I don't know why."

" Then you do like me, Christopher darling ? "

" Yes, of course I like you, Sally. What did you think ? "

" But you're not in love with me, are you ? "

" No. I'm not in love with you."

" I'm awfully glad. I've wanted you to like me ever since we first met. But I'm glad you're not in love with me, because, somehow, I couldn't possibly be in love with you—so, if you had been, everything would have been spoilt."

" Well then, that's very lucky, isn't it ? "

" Yes, very . . ." Sally hesitated. " There's something I want to confess to you, Chris darling. . . . I'm not sure if you'll understand or not."

41

" Remember, I'm only a man, Sally."

Sally laughed: " It's the most idiotic little thing. But somehow, I'd hate it if you found out without my telling you. . . . You know, the other day, you said Fritz had told you my mother was French ? "

" Yes, I remember."

" And I said he must have invented it ? Well, he hadn't. . . . You see, I'd told him she was."

" But why on earth did you do that ? "

We both began to laugh. " Goodness knows," said Sally. " I suppose I wanted to impress him."

" But what is there impressive in having a French mother ? "

" I'm a bit mad like that sometimes, Chris. You must be patient with me."

" All right, Sally, I'll be patient."

" And you'll swear on your honour not to tell Fritz ? "

" I swear."

" If you do, you swine," exclaimed Sally, laughing and picking up the paper-knife dagger from my writing-table, " I'll cut your throat! "

Afterwards, I asked Frl Schroeder what she'd thought of Sally. She was in raptures: " Like a picture, Herr Issyvoo! And so elegant: such beautiful hands and feet! One can see that she belongs to the very best society. . . . You know, Herr Issyvoo, I should never have expected you to have a lady friend like that! You always seem so quiet. . . ."

" Ah, well, Frl Schroeder, it's often the quiet ones——"

She went off into her little scream of

laughter, swaying backwards and for-
wards on her short legs:

" Quite right, Herr Issyvoo! Quite
right! "

.   .   .

On New Year's Eve, Sally came to
live at Frl Schroeder's.

It had all been arranged at the last
moment. Sally, her suspicions sharpened
by my repeated warnings, had caught
out Frau Karpf in a particularly gross
and clumsy piece of swindling. So she
had hardened her heart and given notice.
She was to have Frl Kost's old room.
Frl Schroeder was, of course, enchanted.

We all had our Sylvester Abend
dinner at home: Frl Schroeder, Frl
Mayr, Sally, Bobby, a mixer colleague
from the Troika and myself. It was a
great success. Bobby, already restored

to favour, flirted daringly with Frl
Schroeder. Frl Mayr and Sally, talking
as one great artiste to another, discussed
the possibilities of music-hall work in
England. Sally told some really startling
lies, which she obviously for the moment
half-believed, about how she'd appeared
at the Palladium and the London Coli-
seum. Frl Mayr capped them with a
story of how she'd been drawn through
the streets of Munich in a carriage by
excited students. From this point, it did
not take Sally long to persuade Frl Mayr
to sing *Sennerin Abschied von der Alm*,
which, after claret cup and a bottle of
very inexpensive cognac, so exactly
suited my mood that I shed a few tears.
We all joined in the repeats and the
final, ear-splitting *Juch-he!* Then Sally
sang " I've got those Little Boy Blues "
with so much expression that Bobby's

45

mixer colleague, taking it personally, seized her round the waist and had to be restrained by Bobby, who reminded him firmly that it was time to be getting along to business.

Sally and I went with them to the Troika, where we met Fritz. With him was Klaus Linke, the young pianist who used to accompany Sally when she sang at the Lady Windermere. Later, Fritz and I went off alone. Fritz seemed rather depressed: he wouldn't tell me why. Some girls did classical figure-tableaux behind gauze. And then there was a big dancing-hall with telephones on the tables. We had the usual kind of conversations: " Pardon me, Madame, I feel sure from your voice that you're a fascinating little blonde with long black eyelashes—just my type. How did I know? Aha, that's my secret! Yes—quite right: I'm tall, dark, broad-shouldered, military appearance, and the tiniest little moustache.... You don't believe me ? Then come and see for yourself! " The couples were dancing with hands on each other's hips, yelling in each other's faces, streaming with sweat. An orchestra in Bavarian costume whooped and drank and perspired beer. The place stank like a zoo. After this, I think I strayed off alone and wandered for hours and hours through a jungle of paper streamers. Next morning, when I woke, the bed was full of them.

I had been up and dressed for some time when Sally returned home. She came straight into my room, looking tired but very pleased with herself.

" Hullo, darling! What time is it ? "

" Nearly lunch-time."

" I say, is it really ? How marvellous ! I'm practically starving. I've had nothing for breakfast but a cup of coffee...." She paused expectantly, waiting for my next question.

" Where have you been ? " I asked.

" But, darling," Sally opened her eyes very wide in affected surprise: " I thought you knew! "

" I haven't the least idea."

" Nonsense! "

" Really I haven't, Sally."

" Oh, Christopher darling, how can you be such a liar! Why, it was obvious that you'd planned the whole thing! The way you got rid of Fritz—he looked so cross! Klaus and I nearly died of laughing."

All the same, she wasn't quite at her ease. For the first time, I saw her blush.

" Have you got a cigarette, Chris ? "

I gave her one and lit the match. She blew out a long cloud of smoke and walked slowly to the window:

" I'm most terribly in love with him."

She turned, frowning slightly; crossed to the sofa and curled herself up carefully, arranging her hands and feet: " At least, I think I am," she added.

I allowed a respectful pause to elapse before asking: " And is Klaus in love with you ? "

" He absolutely adores me." Sally was very serious indeed. She smoked for several minutes: " He says he fell in love with me the first time we met, at the Lady Windermere. But as long as we were working together, he didn't dare to say anything. He was afraid it might put me off my singing. . . . He says that, before he met me, he'd no idea what a marvellously beautiful thing a woman's body is. He's only had about three women before, in his life . . ."

I lit a cigarette.

" Of course, Chris, I don't suppose you really understand. . . . It's awfully hard to explain. . . ."

" I'm sure it is."

" I'm seeing him again at four o'clock." Sally's tone was slightly defiant.

" In that case, you'd better get some sleep. I'll ask Frl Schroeder to scramble you some eggs; or I'll do them myself if she's still too drunk. You get into bed. You can eat them there."

" Thanks, Chris darling. You are an angel." Sally yawned. " What on earth I should do without you, I don't know."

.   .   .

After this, Sally and Klaus saw each other every day. They generally met

50

at our house; and, once, Klaus stayed
the whole night. Frl Schroeder didn't
say much to me about it, but I could see
that she was rather shocked. Not that
she disapproved of Klaus: she thought
him very attractive. But she regarded
Sally as my property, and it shocked her
to see me standing so tamely to one side.
I am sure, however, that if I hadn't
known about the affair, and if Sally had
really been deceiving me, Frl Schroeder
would have assisted at the conspiracy
with the greatest relish.

Meanwhile, Klaus and I were a little
shy of each other. When we happened
to meet on the stairs, we bowed coldly
like enemies.

.   .   .

About the middle of January, Klaus
left suddenly, for England. Quite

unexpectedly he had got the offer of a
very good job, synchronizing music
for the films. The afternoon he came
to say good-bye there was a positively
medical atmosphere in the flat, as
though Sally were undergoing a danger-
ous operation. Frl Schroeder and Frl
Mayr sat in the living-room and laid
cards. The results, Frl Schroeder later
assured me, couldn't have been better.
The eight of clubs had appeared three
times in a favourable conjunction.

.　　.　　.

Sally spent the whole of the next
day curled up on the sofa in her room,
with pencil and paper on her lap.
She was writing poems. She wouldn't
let me see them. She smoked cigarette
after cigarette and mixed Prairie
Oysters, but refused to eat more than

a few mouthfuls of Frl Schroeder's omelette.

" Can't I bring you something in, Sally ? "

" No thanks, Chris darling. I just don't want to eat anything at all. I feel all marvellous and ethereal, as if I was a kind of most wonderful saint, or something. You've no idea how glorious it feels. . . . Have a chocolate, darling ? Klaus gave me three boxes. If I eat any more, I shall be sick."

" Thank you."

" I don't suppose I shall ever marry him. It would ruin our careers. You see, Christopher, he adores me so terribly that it wouldn't be good for him to always have me hanging about."

" You might marry after you're both famous."

Sally considered this :

" No. . . . That would spoil everything. We should be trying all the time to live up to our old selves, if you know what I mean. And we should both be different. . . . He was so marvellously primitive: just like a faun. He made me feel like a most marvellous nymph, or something, miles away from anywhere, in the middle of the forest."

.　　　.　　　.

The first letter from Klaus duly arrived. We had all been anxiously awaiting it; and Frl Schroeder woke me up specially early to tell me that it had come. Perhaps she was afraid that she would never get a chance of reading it herself and relied on me to tell her the contents. If so, her fears were groundless. Sally not only showed the letter to Frl Schroeder, Frl Mayr,

Bobby and myself, she even read selections from it aloud in the presence of the porter's wife, who had come up to collect the rent.

From the first, the letter left a nasty taste in my mouth. Its whole tone was egotistical and a bit patronizing. Klaus didn't like London, he said. He felt lonely there. The food disagreed with him. And the people at the studio treated him with lack of consideration. He wished Sally were with him: she could have helped him in many ways. However, now that he was in England, he would try to make the best of it. He would work hard and earn money; and Sally was to work hard too. Work would cheer her up and keep her from getting depressed. At the end of the letter came various endearments, rather too slickly applied. Reading them, one felt: he's written this kind of thing several times before.

Sally was delighted, however. Klaus' exhortation made such an impression upon her that she at once rang up several film companies, a theatrical agency and half a dozen of her "business" acquaintances. Nothing definite came of all this, it is true; but she remained very optimistic throughout the next twenty-four hours—even her dreams, she told me, had been full of contracts and four-figure cheques: "It's the most marvellous feeling, Chris. I know I'm going right ahead now and going to become the most wonderful actress in the world."

.   .   .

One morning, about a week after this, I went into Sally's room and found her holding a letter in her hand. I recognized Klaus' handwriting at once.

" Good morning, Chris darling."

" Good morning, Sally."

" How did you sleep ? " Her tone was unnaturally bright and chatty.

" All right, thanks. How did you ? "

" Fairly all right. . . . Filthy weather isn't it ? "

" Yes." I walked over to the window to look. It was.

Sally smiled conversationally: " Do you know what this swine's gone and done ? "

" What swine ? " I wasn't going to be caught out.

" Oh Chris! For God's sake, don't be so dense! "

" I'm very sorry. I'm afraid I'm a bit slow in the uptake this morning."

" I can't be bothered to explain,

57

darling." Sally held out the letter. " Here, read this, will you ? Of all the blasted impudence! Read it aloud. I want to hear how it sounds."

" Mein liebes, armes Kind," the letter began. Klaus called Sally his poor dear child because, as he explained, he was afraid that what he had to tell her would make her terribly unhappy. Nevertheless, he must say it: he must tell her that he had come to a decision. She mustn't imagine that this had been easy for him: it had been very difficult and painful. All the same, he knew he was right. In a word, they must part.

" I see now," wrote Klaus, " that I behaved very selfishly. I thought only of my own pleasure. But now I realize that I must have had a bad influence on you. My dear little girl, you have adored me too much. If we should continue to be together, you would soon have no will and no mind of your own." Klaus went on to advise Sally to live for her work. "Work is the only thing which matters, as I myself have found." He was very much concerned that Sally shouldn't upset herself unduly: "You must be brave, Sally, my poor darling child."

Right at the end of the letter, it all came out:

"I was invited a few nights ago to a party at the house of Lady Klein, a leader of the English aristocracy. I met there a very beautiful and intelligent young English girl named Miss Gore-Eckersley. She is related to an English lord whose name I couldn't quite hear—you will probably know which one I mean. We have met twice since then and had wonderful conversations about

many things. I do not think I have
ever met a girl who could understand
my mind so well as she does——"

" That's a new one on me," broke in
Sally bitterly, with a short laugh: " I
never suspected the boy of having a
mind at all."

At this moment we were interrupted
by Frl Schroeder who had come,
sniffing secrets, to ask if Sally would
like a bath. I left them together to
make the most of the occasion.

" I can't be angry with the fool,"
said Sally, later in the day, pacing up
and down the room and furiously
smoking: " I just feel sorry for him in
a motherly sort of way. But what on
earth'll happen to *his* work, if he chucks
himself at all these women's heads, I
can't imagine."

She made another turn of the room:

" I think if he'd been having a proper affair with another woman, and had only told me about it after it'd been going on for a long time, I'd have minded more. But this girl! Why, I don't suppose she's even his mistress."

" Obviously not," I agreed. " I say, shall we have a Prairie Oyster ? "

" How marvellous you are, Chris! You always think of just the right thing. I wish I could fall in love with you. Klaus isn't worth your little finger."

" I know he isn't."

" The blasted cheek," exclaimed Sally, gulping the Worcester sauce and licking her upper lip, " of his saying I adored him! . . . The worst of it is, I did! "

That evening I went into her room and found her with pen and paper before her :

61

" I've written about a million letters to him and torn them all up."

" It's no good, Sally. Let's go to the cinema."

" Right you are, Chris darling." Sally wiped her eyes with the corner of her tiny handkerchief: " It's no use bothering, is it ? "

" Not a bit of use."

" And now I jolly well *will* be a great actress—just to show him! "

" That's the spirit! "

We went to a little cinema in the Bülowstrasse, where they were showing a film about a girl who sacrificed her stage career for the sake of a Great Love, Home and Children. We laughed so much that we had to leave before the end.

" I feel ever so much better now," said Sally, as we were coming away.

" I'm glad."

" Perhaps, after all, I can't have been properly in love with him. . . . What do you think ? "

" It's rather difficult for me to say."

" I've often thought I was in love with a man, and then I found I wasn't. But this time," Sally's voice was regretful, " I really did feel *sure* of it. . . . And now, somehow, everything seems to have got a bit confused. . . ."

" Perhaps you're suffering from shock," I suggested.

Sally was very pleased with this idea: " Do you know, I expect I am! . . . You know, Chris, you do understand women most marvellously: better than any man I've ever met. . . . I'm sure that some day you'll write the most marvellous novel which'll sell simply millions of copies."

" Thank you for believing in me, Sally! "

" Do you believe in me, too, Chris ? "

" Of course I do."

" No, but honestly ? "

" Well . . . I'm quite certain you'll make a terrific success at something—only I'm not sure what it'll be. . . . I mean, there's so many things you could do if you tried, aren't there ? "

" I suppose there are." Sally became thoughtful. " At least, sometimes I feel like that. . . . And sometimes I feel I'm no damn' use at anything. . . . Why, I can't even keep a man faithful to me for the inside of a month."

" Oh, Sally, don't let's start all that again! "

" All right, Chris—we won't start all that. Let's go and have a drink."

.   .   .

During the weeks that followed, Sally and I were together most of the day. Curled up on the sofa in the big dingy room, she smoked, drank Prairie Oysters, talked endlessly of the future. When the weather was fine, and I hadn't any lessons to give, we strolled as far as the Wittenbergplatz and sat on a bench in the sunshine, discussing the people who went past. Everybody stared at Sally, in her canary yellow beret and shabby fur coat, like the skin of a mangy old dog.

" I wonder," she was fond of re-marking, " what they'd say if they knew that we two old tramps were going to be the most marvellous

E   65

novelist and the greatest actress in the world."

"They'd probably be very much surprised."

"I expect we shall look back on this time when we're driving about in our Mercedes, and think: After all, it wasn't such bad fun!"

"It wouldn't be such bad fun if we had that Mercedes now."

We talked continually about wealth, fame, huge contracts for Sally, record-breaking sales for the novels I should one day write. "I think," said Sally, "it must be marvellous to be a novelist. You're frightfully dreamy and un-practical and unbusinesslike, and people imagine they can fairly swindle you as much as they want—and then you sit down and write a book about them which fairly shows them what swine they all

are, and it's the most terrific success
and you make pots of money."

" I expect the trouble with me is
that I'm not quite dreamy enough. . . ."

" . . . if only I could get a really
rich man as my lover. Let's see. . . .
I shouldn't want more than three
thousand a year, and a flat and a decent
car. I'd do anything, just now, to get
rich. If you're rich you can afford to
stand out for a really good contract;
you don't have to snap up the first offer
you get. . . . Of course, I'd be absolutely faithful to the man who kept
me——"

Sally said things like this very
seriously and evidently believed she
meant them. She was in a curious state
of mind, restless and nervy. Often she
flew into a temper for no special reason.
She talked incessantly about getting

work, but made no effort to do so. Her allowance hadn't been stopped, so far, however, and we were living very cheaply, since Sally no longer cared to go out in the evenings or to see other people at all. Once, Fritz came to tea. I left them alone together afterwards to go and write a letter. When I came back Fritz had gone and Sally was in tears:

" That man *bores* me so! " she sobbed. " I hate him! I should like to kill him! "

But in a few minutes she was quite calm again. I started to mix the inevitable Prairie Oyster. Sally, curled up on the sofa, was thoughtfully smoking:

" I wonder," she said suddenly, " if I'm going to have a baby."

" Good God! " I nearly dropped the glass: " Do you really think you are ? "

" I don't know. With me it's so difficult to tell: I'm so irregular . . . I've felt sick sometimes. It's probably something I've eaten. . . ."

" But hadn't you better see a doctor ? "

" Oh, I suppose so." Sally yawned listlessly. " There's no hurry."

" Of course there's a hurry! You'll go and see a doctor to-morrow! "

" Look here, Chris, who the hell do you think you're ordering about ? I wish now I hadn't said anything about it at all! " Sally was on the point of bursting into tears again.

" Oh, all right! All right! " I hastily tried to calm her. " Do just what you like. It's no business of mine."

" Sorry, darling. I didn't mean to be snappy. I'll see how I feel in the

69

morning. Perhaps I will go and see that doctor, after all."

But, of course, she didn't. Next day, indeed, she seemed much brighter: " Let's go out this evening, Chris. I'm getting sick of this room. Let's go and see some life! "

" Right you are, Sally. Where would you like to go ? "

" Let's go to the Troika and talk to that old idiot Bobby. Perhaps he'll stand us a drink—you never know! "

Bobby didn't stand us any drinks; but Sally's suggestion proved to have been a good one, nevertheless. For it was while sitting at the bar of the Troika that we first got into conversation with Clive.

．　　　．　　　．

From that moment onwards we were with him almost continuously; either separately or together. I never once saw him sober. Clive told us that he drank half a bottle of whisky before breakfast, and I had no reason to disbelieve him. He often began to explain to us why he drank so much—it was because he was very unhappy. But why he was so unhappy I never found out, because Sally always interrupted to say that it was time to be going out or moving on to the next place or smoking a cigarette or having another glass of whisky. She was drinking nearly as much whisky as Clive himself. It never seemed to make her really drunk, but sometimes her eyes looked awful, as though they had been boiled. Every day the layer of make-up on her face seemed to get thicker.

Clive was a very big man, good-looking in a heavy Roman way, and

just beginning to get fat. He had about
him that sad, American air of vagueness
which is always attractive; doubly
attractive in one who possessed so much
money. He was vague, wistful, a bit
lost: dimly anxious to have a good
time and uncertain how to set about
getting it. He seemed never to be quite
sure whether he was really enjoying
himself, whether what we were doing
was *really* fun. He had constantly to be
reassured. *Was* this the genuine article?
Was this the real guaranteed height of
a Good Time? It was? Yes, yes, of
course—it was marvellous! It was
great! Ha, ha, ha! His big school-
boyish laugh rolled out, re-echoed,
became rather forced and died away
abruptly on that puzzled note of
enquiry. He couldn't venture a step
without our support. Yet, even as he

appealed to us, I thought I could sometimes detect odd sly flashes of sarcasm.
What did he really think of us?

Every morning, Clive sent round a
hired car to fetch us to the hotel where
he was staying. The chauffeur always
brought with him a wonderful bouquet
of flowers, ordered from the most
expensive flower-shop in the Linden.
One morning I had a lesson to give and
arranged with Sally to join them later.
On arriving at the hotel, I found that
Clive and Sally had left early to fly to
Dresden. There was a note from Clive,
apologizing profusely and inviting me
to lunch at the hotel restaurant, by
myself, as his guest. But I didn't. I
was afraid of that look in the head
waiter's eye. In the evening, when
Clive and Sally returned, Clive had
brought me a present: it was a parcel

of six silk shirts. " He wanted to get you a gold cigarette case," Sally whispered in my ear, " but I told him shirts would be better. Yours are in such a state. . . . Besides, we've got to go slow at present. We don't want him to think we're gold-diggers. . . ."

I accepted them gratefully. What else could I do ? Clive had corrupted us utterly. It was understood that he was going to put down the money to launch Sally upon a stage career. He often spoke of this, in a thoroughly nice way, as though it were a very trivial matter, to be settled, without fuss, between friends. But no sooner had he touched on the subject than his attention seemed to wander off again—his thoughts were as easily distracted as those of a child. Sometimes Sally was very hard put to it, I could see, to hide her impatience. " Just leave us alone for a bit now, darling," she would whisper to me, " Clive and I are going to talk business." But however tactfully Sally tried to bring him to the point, she never quite succeeded. When I rejoined them, half an hour later, I would find Clive smiling and sipping his whisky; and Sally also smiling, to conceal her extreme irritation.

" I adore him," Sally told me, repeatedly and very solemnly, whenever we were alone together. She was intensely earnest in believing this. It was like a dogma in a newly adopted religious creed: Sally adores Clive. It is a very solemn undertaking to adore a millionaire. Sally's features began to assume, with increasing frequency, the rapt expression of the theatrical nun. And indeed, when Clive, with his charming vagueness, gave a particularly flagrant professional beggar a twenty-mark note, we would exchange glances of genuine awe. The waste of so much good money affected us both like something inspired, a kind of miracle.

.　　　.　　　.

There came an afternoon when Clive seemed more nearly sober than usual. He began to make plans. In a few days we were all three of us to leave Berlin, for good. The Orient Express would take us to Athens. Thence, we should fly to Egypt. From Egypt to Marseille. From Marseille, by boat to South America. Then Tahiti. Singapore. Japan. Clive pronounced the names as though they had been stations on the Wannsee railway, quite as a matter of course: he had been there already. He knew it all. His matter-of-fact boredom gradually infused reality into the preposterous conversation. After all, he could do it. I began seriously to believe that he meant to do it. With a mere gesture of his wealth, he could alter the whole course of our lives.

What would become of us ? Once started, we should never go back. We could never leave him. Sally, of course, he would marry. I should occupy an ill-defined position: a kind of private secretary without duties. With a flash of vision, I saw myself ten years hence, in flannels and black and white shoes, gone heavier round the jowl and a bit glassy, pouring out a drink in the lounge of a Californian hotel.

" Come and cast an eye at the funeral," Clive was saying.

" What funeral, darling ? " Sally

77

asked, patiently. This was a new kind
of interruption.

" Why, say, haven't you noticed
it ? " Clive laughed. " It's a most
elegant funeral. It's been going past
for the last hour."

We all three went out on to the
balcony of Clive's room. Sure enough,
the street below was full of people.
They were burying Hermann Müller.
Ranks of pale steadfast clerks, govern-
ment officials, trade union secretaries—
the whole drab weary pageant of Prussian
Social Democracy—trudged past under
their banners towards the silhouetted
arches of the Brandenburger Tor, from
which the long black streamers stirred
slowly in an evening breeze.

" Say, who was this guy, anyway ? "
asked Clive, looking down. " I guess
he must have been a big swell ? "

" God knows," Sally answered, yawning. " Look, Clive darling, isn't it a marvellous sunset ? "

She was quite right. We had nothing to do with those Germans down there, marching, or with the dead man in the coffin, or with the words on the banners. In a few days, I thought, we shall have forfeited all kinship with ninety-nine per cent. of the population of the world, with the men and women who earn their living, who insure their lives, who are anxious about the future of their children. Perhaps in the Middle Ages people felt like this, when they believed themselves to have sold their souls to the Devil. It was a curious, exhilarating, not unpleasant sensation: but, at the same time, I felt slightly scared. Yes, I said to myself, I've done it, now. I am lost.

Next morning, we arrived at the hotel at the usual time. The porter eyed us, I thought, rather queerly.

"Whom did you wish to see, Madam?"

The question seemed so extraordinary that we both laughed.

"Why, number 365, of course," Sally answered. "Who did you think? Don't you know us by this time?"

"I'm afraid you can't do that, Madam. The gentleman in 365 left early this morning."

"Left? You mean he's gone out for the day? That's funny! What time will he be back?"

"He didn't say anything about coming back, Madam. He was travelling to Budapest."

As we stood there goggling at him, a waiter hurried up with a note.

" Dear Sally and Chris," it said, " I can't stick this darned town any longer, so am off. Hoping to see you some-time, Clive.

"(These are in case I forgot any-thing.)"

In the envelope were three hundred-mark notes. These, the fading flowers, Sally's four pairs of shoes and two hats (bought in Dresden) and my six shirts were our total assets from Clive's visit. At first, Sally was very angry. Then we both began to laugh:

" Well, Chris, I'm afraid we're not much use as gold-diggers, are we, darling ? "

We spent most of the day discussing whether Clive's departure was a pre-meditated trick. I was inclined to think it wasn't. I imagined him leaving every new town and every new set of

F   81

acquaintances in much the same sort of way. I sympathized with him, a good deal.

Then came the question of what was to be done with the money. Sally decided to put by two hundred and fifty marks for some new clothes: fifty marks we would blow that evening.

But blowing the fifty marks wasn't as much fun as we'd imagined it would be. Sally felt ill and couldn't eat the wonderful dinner we'd ordered. We were both depressed.

" You know, Chris, I'm beginning to think that men are always going to leave me. The more I think about it, the more men I remember who have. It's ghastly, really."

" I'll never leave you, Sally."

" Won't you, darling ? . . . But seriously, I believe I'm a sort of Ideal

Woman, if you know what I mean. I'm the sort of woman who can take men away from their wives, but I could never keep anybody for long. And that's because I'm the type which every man imagines he wants, until he gets me; and then he finds he doesn't really, after all."

" Well, you'd rather be that than the Ugly Duckling with the Heart of Gold, wouldn't you ? "

" . . . I could kick myself, the way I behaved to Clive. I ought never to have bothered him about money, the way I did. I expect he thought I was just a common little whore, like all the others. And I really did adore him—in a way. . . . If I'd married him, I'd have made a man out of him. I'd have got him to give up drinking."

" You set him such a good example."

We both laughed.

" The old swine might at least have left me with a decent cheque."

" Never mind, darling. There's more where he came from."

" I don't care," said Sally. " I'm sick of being a whore. I'll never look at a man with money again."

·   ·

Next morning, Sally felt very ill. We both put it down to the drink. She stayed in bed the whole morning and when she got up she fainted. I wanted her to see a doctor straight away, but she wouldn't. About tea-time, she fainted again and looked so bad afterwards that Frl Schroeder and I sent for a doctor without consulting her at all.

The doctor, when he arrived, stayed a long time. Frl Schroeder and I sat waiting in the living-room to hear his diagnosis. But, very much to our surprise, he left the flat suddenly, in a great hurry, without even looking in to wish us good afternoon. I went at once to Sally's room. Sally was sitting up in bed, with a rather fixed grin on her face:

" Well, Christopher darling, I've been made an April Fool of."

" What do you mean ? "

Sally tried to laugh :

" He says I'm going to have a baby."

" Oh my God! "

" Don't look so scared, darling! I've been more or less expecting it, you know."

" It's Klaus's, I suppose ? "

" Yes."

" And what are you going to do about it ? "

" Not have it, of course." Sally reached for a cigarette. I sat stupidly staring at my shoes.

" Will the doctor . . ."

" No, he won't. I asked him straight out. He was terribly shocked. I said ' My dear man, what do you imagine would happen to the unfortunate child if it was born ? Do I look as if I'd make a good mother ? ' "

" And what did he say to that ? "

" He seemed to think it was quite beside the point. The only thing which matters to him is his professional reputation."

" Well then, we've got to find someone without a professional reputation, that's all."

" I should think," said Sally, " we'd better ask Frl Schroeder."

So Frl Schroeder was consulted. She

took it very well: she was alarmed but extremely practical. Yes, she knew of somebody. A friend of a friend's friend had once had difficulties. And the doctor was a fully qualified man, very clever indeed. The only trouble was, he might be rather expensive.

"Thank goodness," Sally interjected, "we haven't spent all that swine Clive's money!"

"I must say, I think Klaus ought——"

"Look here, Chris. Let me tell you this once for all: if I catch you writing to Klaus about this business, I'll never forgive you and I'll never speak to you again!"

"Oh, very well . . . Of course I won't. It was just a suggestion, that's all."

I didn't like the doctor. He kept

stroking and pinching Sally's arm and pawing her hand. However, he seemed the right man for the job. Sally was to go into his private nursing-home as soon as there was a vacancy for her. Everything was perfectly official and above-board. In a few polished sentences, the dapper little doctor dispelled the least whiff of sinister illegality. Sally's state of health, he explained, made it quite impossible for her to undergo the risks of childbirth: there would be a certificate to that effect. Needless to say, the certificate would cost a lot of money. So would the nursing-home and so would the operation itself. The doctor wanted two hundred and fifty marks down before he would make any arrangements at all. In the end, we beat him down to two hundred. Sally wanted the extra fifty, she explained to me later, to get some new nightdresses.

.   .   .

At last, it was spring. The cafés were putting up wooden platforms on the pavement and the ice-cream shops were opening, with their rainbow-wheels. We drove to the nursing-home in an open taxi. Because of the lovely weather, Sally was in better spirits than I had seen her in for weeks. But Frl Schroeder, though she bravely tried to smile, was on the verge of tears. "The doctor isn't a Jew, I hope?" Frl Mayr asked me sternly. "Don't you let one of those filthy Jews touch her. They always try to get a job of that kind, the beasts!"

Sally had a nice room, clean and cheerful, with a balcony. I called there again in the evening. Lying there in bed without her make-up, she looked years younger, like a little girl:

" Hullo, darling. . . . They haven't killed me yet, you see. But they've been doing their best to. . . . Isn't this a funny place ? . . . I wish that pig Klaus could see me. . . . This is what comes of not understanding his mind. . . ."

She was a bit feverish and laughed a great deal. One of the nurses came in for a moment, as if looking for something, and went out again almost immediately.

" She was dying to get a peep at you," Sally explained. " You see, I told her you were the father. You don't mind, do you, darling . . ."

" Not at all. It's a compliment."

" It makes everything so much simpler. Otherwise, if there's no one, they think it so odd. And I don't care for being sort of looked down on and pitied as the poor betrayed girl who gets abandoned by her lover. It isn't particularly flattering for me, is it? So I told her we were most terribly in love but fearfully hard up, so that we couldn't afford to marry, and how we dreamed of the time when we'd both be rich and famous and then we'd have a family of ten, just to make up for this one. The nurse was awfully touched, poor girl. In fact, she wept. To-night, when she's on duty, she's going to show me pictures of *her* young man. Isn't it sweet?"

.   .   .

Next day, Frl Schroeder and I went round to the nursing-home together. We found Sally lying flat, with the bedclothes up to her chin:

"Oh, hullo, you two! Won't you sit down? What time is it?" She turned uneasily in bed and rubbed her eyes: "Where did all these flowers come from?"

"We brought them."

"How marvellous of you!" Sally smiled vacantly. "Sorry to be such a fool to-day. . . . It's this bloody chloroform. . . . My head's full of it."

We only stayed a few minutes. On the way home, Frl Schroeder was terribly upset: "Will you believe it, Herr Issyvoo, I couldn't take it more to heart if it was my own daughter? Why, when I see the poor child suffering like that, I'd rather it was myself lying there in her place—I would indeed!"

Next day Sally was much better. We all went to visit her: Frl Schroeder,

Frl Mayr, Bobby and Fritz. Fritz, of course, hadn't the faintest idea what had really happened. Sally, he had been told, was being operated upon for a small internal ulcer. As always is the way with people when they aren't in the know, he made all kinds of unintentional and startlingly apt references to storks, gooseberry-bushes, perambulators and babies generally; and even recounted a special new item of scandal about a well-known Berlin society lady who was said to have undergone a recent illegal operation. Sally and I avoided each other's eyes.

.   .   .

On the evening of the next day, I visited her at the nursing-home for the last time. She was to leave in the morning. She was alone and we sat together

on the balcony. She seemed more or
less all right now and could walk about
the room.

"I told the Sister I didn't want to
see anybody to-day except you." Sally
yawned languidly. "People make me
feel so tired."

"Would you rather I went away
too?"

"Oh no," said Sally, without much
enthusiasm, "if you go, one of the
nurses will only come in and begin to
chatter; and if I'm not lively and bright
with her, they'll say I have to stay in
this hellish place a couple of extra days,
and I couldn't stand that."

She stared out moodily over the
quiet street:

"You know, Chris, in some ways I
wish I'd had that kid. . . . It would
have been rather marvellous to have had

it. The last day or two, I've been sort of feeling what it would be like to be a mother. Do you know, last night, I sat here for a long time by myself and held this cushion in my arms and imagined it was my baby? And I felt a most marvellous sort of shut-off feeling from all the rest of the world. I imagined how it'd grow up and how I'd work for it, and how, after I'd put it to bed at nights, I'd go out and make love to filthy old men to get money to pay for its food and clothes. . . . It's all very well for you to grin like that, Chris . . . I did really!"

"Well, why don't you marry and have one?"

"I don't know. . . . I feel as if I'd lost faith in men. I just haven't any use for them at all. . . . Even you, Christopher, if you were to go out into

95

the street now and be run over by a taxi. . . . I should be sorry in a way, of course, but I shouldn't really *care* a damn."

" Thank you, Sally."

We both laughed.

" I didn't mean that, of course, darling—at least, not personally. You mustn't mind what I say while I'm like this. I get all sorts of crazy ideas into my head. Having babies makes you feel awfully primitive, like a sort of wild animal or something, defending its young. Only the trouble is, I haven't any young to defend. . . . I expect that's what makes me so frightfully bad-tempered to everybody just now."

. . .

It was partly as the result of this conversation that I suddenly decided, that evening, to cancel all my lessons, leave Berlin as soon as possible, go to some place on the Baltic and try to start working. Since Christmas, I had hardly written a word.

Sally, when I told her my idea, was rather relieved, I think. We both needed a change. We talked vaguely of her joining me later; but, even then, I felt that she wouldn't. Her plans were very uncertain. Later, she might go to Paris, or to the Alps, or to the South of France, she said—if she could get the cash. " But probably," she added, " I shall just stay on here. I should be quite happy. I seem to have got sort of used to this place."

.   .   .

I returned to Berlin towards the middle of July.

All this time I had heard nothing of Sally, beyond half a dozen postcards, exchanged during the first month of my absence. I wasn't much surprised to find she'd left her room in our flat:

"Of course, I quite understand her going. I couldn't make her as comfortable as she'd the right to expect; especially as we haven't any running water in the bedrooms." Poor Frl Schroeder's eyes had filled with tears. "But it was a terrible disappointment to me, all the same. . . . Frl Bowles behaved very handsomely, I can't complain about that. She insisted on paying for her room until the end of July. I was entitled to the money, of course, because she didn't give notice until the twenty-first—but I'd never have mentioned it. . . . She was such a charming young lady——"

" Have you got her address ? "

" Oh yes, and the telephone number. You'll be ringing her up, of course. She'll be delighted to see you. . . . The other gentlemen came and went, but you were her real friend, Herr Issyvoo. You know, I always used to hope that you two would get married. You'd have made an ideal couple. You always had such a good steady influence on her, and she used to brighten you up a bit when you got too deep in your books and studies. . . . Oh yes, Herr Issyvoo, you may laugh—but you never can tell ! Perhaps it isn't too late yet ! "

. . .

Next morning, Frl Schroeder woke me in great excitement:

" Herr Issyvoo, what do you think !

They've shut the Darmstädter und
National! There'll be thousands ruined,
I shouldn't wonder! The milkman says
we'll have civil war in a fortnight!
Whatever do you say to that! "

As soon as I'd got dressed, I went
down into the street. Sure enough,
there was a crowd outside the branch
bank on the Nollendorfplatz corner, a
lot of men with leather satchels and
women with string-bags—women like
Frl Schroeder herself. The iron lattices
were drawn down over the bank win-
dows. Most of the people were staring
intently and rather stupidly at the
locked door. In the middle of the door
was fixed a small notice, beautifully
printed in gothic type, like a page from
a classic author. The notice said that
the Reichspresident had guaranteed the
deposits. Everything was quite all

right. Only the bank wasn't going to open.

A little boy was playing with a hoop amongst the crowd. The hoop ran against a woman's legs. She flew out at him at once: " Du, sei bloss nicht so frech! Cheeky little brat! What do you want here!" Another woman joined in, attacking the scared boy: " Get out! You can't understand it, can you ?" And another asked, in furious sarcasm: " Have you got your money in the bank too, perhaps ?" The boy fled before their pent-up, exploding rage.

In the afternoon it was very hot. The details of the new emergency decrees were in the early evening papers— terse, governmentally inspired. One alarmist headline stood out boldly, barred with blood-red ink: " Everything Collapses!" A Nazi journalist reminded his readers that to-morrow, the fourteenth of July, was a day of national rejoicing in France; and doubtless, he added, the French would rejoice with especial fervour this year, at the prospect of Germany's downfall. Going into an outfitter's, I bought myself a pair of ready-made flannel trousers for twelve marks fifty—a gesture of confidence by England. Then I got into the Underground to go and visit Sally.

She was living in a block of three-room flats, designed as an Artists' Colony, not far from the Breitenbach-platz. When I rang the bell, she opened the door to me herself:

" Hillooo, Chris, you old swine! "

" Hullo, Sally darling! "

" How are you ? . . . Be careful, darling, you'll make me untidy. I've got to go out in a few minutes."

I had never seen her all in white before. It suited her. But her face looked thinner and older. Her hair was cut in a new way and beautifully waved.

" You're very smart," I said.

" Am I ? " Sally smiled her pleased, dreamy, self-conscious smile. I followed her into the sitting-room of the flat. One wall was entirely window. There was some cherry-coloured wooden furniture and a very low divan with gaudy fringed cushions. A fluffy white miniature dog jumped to its feet and yapped. Sally picked it up and went through the gestures of kissing it, just not touching it with her lips:

" Freddi, mein Liebling, Du bist *soo* suss ! "

" Yours ? " I asked, noticing the improvement in her German accent.

" No. He belongs to Gerda, the girl I share this flat with."

" Have you known her long ? "

" Only a week or two."

" What's she like ? "

" Not bad. As stingy as hell. I have to pay for practically everything."

" It's nice here."

" Do you think so ? Yes, I suppose it's all right. Better than that hole in the Nollendorfstrasse, anyhow."

" What made you leave ? Did you and Frl Schroeder have a row ? "

" No, not exactly. Only I got so sick of hearing her talk. She nearly talked my head off. She's an awful old bore, really."

" She's very fond of you."

Sally shrugged her shoulders with a slight impatient listless movement. Throughout this conversation, I noticed

that she avoided my eyes. There was a
long pause. I felt puzzled and vaguely
embarrassed. I began to wonder how
soon I could make an excuse to go.

Then the telephone bell rang. Sally
yawned, pulled the instrument across on
to her lap:

"Hilloo, who's there? Yes, it's
me. . . . No. . . . No. . . . I've really
no idea. . . . *Really* I haven't! I'm to
guess!" Her nose wrinkled: "Is it
Erwin? No? Paul? No? Wait a
minute. . . . Let me see. . . ."

"And now, darling, I must fly!"
cried Sally, when, at last, the conversation was over: "I'm about two hours
late already!"

"Got a new boy friend?"

But Sally ignored my grin. She lit
a cigarette with a faint expression of
distaste.

" I've got to see a man on business,"
she said briefly.

" And when shall we meet again ? "

" I'll have to see, darling. . . . I've
got such a lot on, just at present. . . .
I shall be out in the country all day
to-morrow and probably the day after.
. . . I'll let you know. . . . I may be
going to Frankfurt quite soon."

" Have you got a job there ? "

" No. Not exactly." Sally's voice
was brief, dismissing this subject. " I've
decided not to try for any film work
until the autumn, anyhow. I shall take
a thorough rest."

" You seem to have made a lot of new
friends."

Again, Sally's manner became vague,
carefully casual :

" Yes, I suppose I have. . . . It's
probably a reaction from all those

months at Frl Schroeder's, when I
never saw a soul."

"Well," I couldn't resist a malicious
grin, "I hope for your sake that none
of your new friends have got their
money in the Darmstädter und
National."

"Why?" She was interested at
once. "What's the matter with
it?"

"Do you really mean to say you
haven't heard?"

"Of course not. I never read the
papers, and I haven't been out to-day,
yet."

I told her the news of the crisis. At
the end of it, she was looking quite
scared.

"But why on earth," she exclaimed
impatiently, "didn't you tell me all this
before? It may be serious."

" I'm sorry, Sally. I took it for granted that you'd know already . . . especially as you seem to be moving in financial circles, nowadays——"

But she ignored this little dig. She was frowning, deep in her own thoughts :

" If it was *very* serious, Leo would have rung up and told me . . ." she murmured at length. And this reflection appeared to ease her mind considerably.

We walked out together to the corner of the street, where Sally picked up a taxi.

" It's an awful nuisance living so far off," she said. " I'm probably going to get a car, soon."

" By the way," she added, just as we were parting, " what was it like in Rügen ? "

" I bathed a lot."

" Well, good-bye, darling. I'll see you sometime."

" Good-bye, Sally. Enjoy yourself."

. . .

About a week after this, Sally rang me up:

" Can you come round at once, Chris ? It's very important. I want you to do me a favour."

This time, also, I found Sally alone in the flat.

" Do you want to earn some money, darling ? " she greeted me.

" Of course."

" Splendid ! You see, it's like this. . . ." She was in a fluffy pink dressing-wrap and inclined to be breathless: " There's a man I know who's starting a magazine. It's going to be most terribly high-brow and artistic, with lots of marvellous modern photographs, ink-pots and girls' heads upside down —you know the sort of thing. . . . The point is, each number is going to take a special country and kind of review it, with articles about the manners and customs, and all that. . . . Well, the first country they're going to do is England and they want me to write an article on the English Girl. . . . Of course, I haven't the foggiest idea what to say, so what I thought was: you could write the article in my name and get the money—I only want not to disoblige this man who's editing the paper, because he may be terribly useful to me in other ways, later on. . . ."

"All right, I'll try."

"Oh, marvellous!"

"How soon do you want it done?"

"You see, darling, that's the whole point. I must have it at once. . . . Otherwise it's no earthly use, because I promised it four days ago and I simply must give it him this evening. . . . It needn't be very long. About five hundred words."

"Well, I'll do my best. . . ."

"Good. That's wonderful. . . . Sit down wherever you like. Here's some paper. You've got a pen? Oh, and here's a dictionary, in case there's a word you can't spell. . . . I'll just be having my bath."

When, three-quarters of an hour later, Sally came in dressed for the day, I had finished. Frankly, I was rather pleased with my effort.

She read it through carefully, a slow frown gathering between her beautifully pencilled eyebrows. When she had finished, she laid down the manuscript with a sigh:

" I'm sorry, Chris. It won't do at all."

" Won't do ? " I was genuinely taken aback.

" Of course, I dare say it's very good from a literary point of view, and all that. . . ."

" Well then, what's wrong with it ? "

" It's not nearly snappy enough." Sally was quite final. " It's not the kind of thing this man wants, at all."

I shrugged my shoulders: " I'm sorry, Sally. I did my best. But journalism isn't really in my line, you know."

There was a resentful pause. My vanity was piqued.

" My goodness, I know who'll do it for me if I ask him! " cried Sally,

suddenly jumping up. " Why on earth
didn't I think of him before ? " She
grabbed the telephone and dialled a
number: " Oh, hilloo, Kurt darling.
. . ."

In three minutes, she had explained
all about the article. Replacing the
receiver on its stand, she announced
triumphantly: " That's marvellous!
He's going to do it at once. . . ."
She paused impressively and added:
" That was Kurt Rosenthal."

" Who's he ? "

" You've never heard of him ? "
This annoyed Sally; she pretended to
be immensely surprised: " I thought
you took an interest in the cinema ?
He's miles the best young scenario
writer. He earns pots of money. He's
only doing this as a favour to me, of
course. . . . He says he'll dictate it

H   113

to his secretary while he's shaving and then send it straight round to the editor's flat. . . . He's marvellous!"

" Are you sure it'll be what the editor wants, this time ? "

" Of course it will! Kurt's an absolute genius. He can do anything. Just now, he's writing a novel in his spare time. He's so fearfully busy, he can only dictate it while he's having breakfast. He showed me the first few chapters, the other day. Honestly, I think it's easily the best novel I've ever read."

" Indeed ? "

" That's the sort of writer I admire," Sally continued. She was careful to avoid my eye. " He's terribly ambitious and he works the whole time; and he can write anything—anything you like: scenarios, novels, plays, poetry, advertisements. . . . He's not a bit stuck-up about it either. Not like these young men who, because they've written one book, start talking about Art and imagining they're the most wonderful authors in the world. . . . They make me sick. . . ."

Irritated as I was with her, I couldn't help laughing:

"Since when have you disapproved of me so violently, Sally?"

"I don't disapprove of you"—but she couldn't look me in the face—"not exactly."

"I merely make you sick?"

"I don't know what it is. . . . You seem to have changed, somehow. . . ."

"How have I changed?"

"It's difficult to explain. . . . You don't seem to have any energy or want to get anywhere. You're so dilettante. It annoys me."

" I'm sorry." But my would-be facetious tone sounded rather forced. Sally frowned down at her tiny black shoes.

" You must remember I'm a woman, Christopher. All women like men to be strong and decided and following out their careers. A woman wants to be motherly to a man and protect his weak side, but he must have a strong side too, which she can respect. . . . If you ever care for a woman, I don't advise you to let her see that you've got no ambition. Otherwise she'll get to despise you."

" Yes, I see. . . . And that's the principle on which you choose your friends—your *new* friends ? "

She flared up at this:

" It's very easy for you to sneer at my friends for having good business heads. If they've got money, it's because they've worked for it. . . . I suppose you consider yourself better than they are ? "

" Yes, Sally, since you ask me—if they're at all as I imagine them—I do."

" There you go, Christopher! That's typical of you. That's what annoys me about you: you're conceited and lazy. If you say things like that, you ought to be able to prove them."

" How does one prove that one's better than somebody else ? Besides, that's not what I said. I said I considered myself better—it's simply a matter of taste."

Sally made no reply. She lit a cigarette, slightly frowning.

" You say I seem to have changed,"

I continued. " To be quite frank, I've been thinking the same thing about *you*."

Sally didn't seem surprised: " Have you, Christopher ? Perhaps you're right. I don't know. . . . Or perhaps we've neither of us changed. Perhaps we're just seeing each other as we really are. We're awfully different in lots of ways, you know."

" Yes, I've noticed that."

" I think," said Sally, smoking meditatively, her eyes on her shoes, " that we may have sort of outgrown each other, a bit."

" Perhaps we have. . . ." I smiled: Sally's real meaning was so obvious: " At any rate, we needn't quarrel about it, need we ? "

" Of course not, darling."

There was a pause. Then I said that

I must be going. We were both rather embarrassed, now, and extra polite.

" Are you certain you won't have a cup of coffee ? "

" No, thanks awfully."

" Have some tea ? It's specially good. I got it as a present."

" No, thanks very much indeed, Sally. I really must be getting along."

" Must you ? " She sounded, after all, rather relieved. " Be sure and ring me up some time soon, won't you ? "

" Yes, rather."

.   .   .

It wasn't until I had actually left the house and was walking quickly away up the street that I realized how angry and ashamed I felt. What an utter little bitch she is, I thought. After all, I told myself, it's only what I've always

known she was like—right from the
start. No, that wasn't true: I hadn't
known it. I'd flattered myself—why
not be frank about it?—that she was
fond of me. Well, I'd been wrong, it
seemed; but could I blame her for
that? Yet I did blame her, I was
furious with her; nothing would have
pleased me more, at that moment, than
to see her soundly whipped. Indeed, I
was so absurdly upset that I began to
wonder whether I hadn't, all this time,
in my own peculiar way, been in love
with Sally myself.

But no, it wasn't love either—it was
worse. It was the cheapest, most
childish kind of wounded vanity. Not
that I cared a curse what she thought of
my article—well, just a little, perhaps,
but only a very little; my literary self-
conceit was proof against anything *she*

could say—it was her criticism of myself. The awful sexual flair women have for taking the stuffing out of a man! It was no use telling myself that Sally had the vocabulary and mentality of a twelve-year-old schoolgirl, that she was altogether comic and preposterous; it was no use—I only knew that I'd been somehow made to feel a sham. Wasn't I a bit of a sham anyway— though not for her ridiculous reasons— with my arty talk to lady pupils and my newly-acquired parlour-socialism? Yes, I was. But she knew nothing about that. I could quite easily have impressed her. That was the most humiliating part of the whole business; I had mis-managed our interview from the very beginning. I had blushed and squabbled, instead of being wonderful, convincing, superior, fatherly, mature. I had tried to compete with her beastly little Kurt on his own ground; just the very thing, of course, which Sally had wanted and expected me to do! After all these months, I had made the one really fatal mistake——I had let her see that I was not only incompetent but jealous. Yes, vulgarly jealous. I could have kicked myself. The mere thought made me prickly with shame from head to foot.

Well, the mischief was done, now. There was only one thing for it, and that was to forget the whole affair. And of course it would be impossible for me ever to see Sally again.

.   .   .

It must have been about ten days after this that I was visited, one morning, by a small pale dark-haired young man who spoke American fluently with a slight foreign accent. His name, he told me, was George P. Sandars. He had seen my English-teaching advertisement in the B.Z. am Mittag.

" When would you like to begin ? " I asked him.

But the young man shook his head hastily. Oh no, he hadn't come to take lessons, at all. Rather disappointed, I waited politely for him to explain the reason of his visit. He seemed in no hurry to do this. Instead, he accepted a cigarette, sat down and began to talk chattily about the States. Had I ever been to Chicago ? No ? Well, had I heard of James L. Schraube ? I hadn't ? The young man uttered a faint sigh. He had the air of being very patient with me, and with the world in general. He had evidently been over the same ground with a good many other people already. James L. Schraube, he explained, was a very big man in Chicago: he owned a whole chain of restaurants and several cinemas. He had two large country houses and a yacht on Lake Michigan. And he possessed no less than four cars. By this time, I was beginning to drum with my fingers on the table. A pained expression passed over the young man's face. He excused himself for taking up my valuable time; he had only told me about Mr. Schraube, he said, because he thought I might be interested—his tone implied a gentle rebuke—and because Mr. Schraube, had I known him, would certainly have vouched for his friend Sandars' respectability. However . . . it couldn't be helped . . . well, would I lend him two hundred marks? He needed the money in order to start a business; it was a unique opportunity, which he would miss altogether if he didn't find the money before to-morrow morning. He would pay me back within three days. If I gave him the money now he would return that same evening with papers to prove that the whole thing was perfectly genuine.

No ? Ah well. . . . He didn't seem unduly surprised. He rose to go at once, like a business man who has wasted a valuable twenty minutes on a prospective customer : the loss, he contrived politely to imply, was mine, not his. Already at the door, he paused for a moment: Did I happen, by any chance, to know some film actresses ? He was travelling, as a sideline, in a new kind of face-cream specially invented to keep the skin from getting dried up by the studio lights. It was being used by all the Hollywood stars already, but in Europe it was still quite unknown. If he could find half a dozen actresses to use and recommend it, they should have free sample jars and permanent supplies at half-price.

After a moment's hesitation, I gave him Sally's address. I don't know quite why I did it. Partly, of course, to get rid of the young man, who showed signs of wishing to sit down again and continue our conversation. Partly, perhaps, out of malice. It would do Sally no harm to have to put up with his chatter for an hour or two: she had told me that she liked men with ambition. Perhaps she would even get a jar of the face-cream—if it existed at all. And if he touched her for the two hundred marks—well, that wouldn't matter so very much, either. He couldn't deceive a baby.

" But whatever you do," I warned him, " don't say that I sent you."

He agreed to this at once, with a slight smile. He must have had his own explanation of my request, for he didn't appear to find it in the least strange. He raised his hat politely as he went downstairs. By the next morning, I had forgotten about his visit altogether.

.   .   .

A few days later, Sally herself rang me up. I had been called away in the middle of a lesson to answer the telephone and was very ungracious.

" Oh, is that you, Christopher darling ? "

" Yes. It's me."

" I say, can you come round and see me at once ? "

" No."

" Oh. . . ." My refusal evidently gave Sally a shock. There was a little pause, then she continued, in a tone of unwonted humility: " I suppose you're most terribly busy ? "

" Yes. I am."

" Well . . . would you mind frightfully if I came round to see you? "

" What about ? "

" Darling "—Sally sounded positively desperate—" I can't possibly explain to you over the telephone. . . . It's something really serious."

" Oh, I see "—I tried to make this as nasty as possible—" another magazine article, I suppose ? "

Nevertheless, as soon as I'd said it, we both had to laugh.

128

" Chris, you are a brute! " Sally
tinkled gaily along the wire: then
checked herself abruptly: " No, darling
—this time I promise you: it's most
terribly serious, really and truly it is."
She paused; then impressively added:
" And you're the only person who can
possibly help."

" Oh, all right. . . ." I was more
than half melted already. " Come in an
hour."

.   .   .

" Well, darling, I'll begin at the
very beginning, shall I ? . . . Yester-
day morning, a man rang me up and
asked if he could come round and see
me. He said it was on very important
business; and as he seemed to know
my name and everything of course I
said: Yes, certainly, come at once. . . .

So he came. He told me his name was
Rakowski—Paul Rakowski—and that
he was a European agent of Metro-
Goldwyn-Mayer and that he'd come to
make me an offer. He said they were
looking out for an English actress who
spoke German to act in a comedy film
they were going to shoot on the Italian
Riviera. He was most frightfully convincing about it all; he told me who the
director was and the camera-man and
the art-director and who'd written the
script. Naturally, I hadn't heard of any
of them before. But that didn't seem so
surprising: in fact, it really made it
sound much more real, because most
people would have chosen one of the
names you see in the newspapers. . . .
Anyhow, he said that, now he'd seen me,
he was sure I'd be just the person for
the part, and he could practically

promise it to me, as long as the test was all right . . . so of course I was simply thrilled and I asked when the test would be and he said not for a day or two, as he had to make arrangements with the Ufa people. . . . So then we began to talk about Hollywood and he told me all kinds of stories—I suppose they *could* have been things he'd read in fan magazines, but somehow I'm pretty sure they weren't—and then he told me how they make sound-effects and how they do the trick-work; he was really most awfully interesting and he certainly must have been inside a great many studios. . . . Anyhow, when we'd finished talking about Hollywood, he started to tell me about the rest of America and the people he knew, and about the gangsters and about New York. He said he'd only just arrived from there and all his luggage was still in the customs at Hamburg. As a matter of fact, I *had* been thinking to myself that it seemed rather queer he was so shabbily dressed; but after he said that, of course, I thought it was quite natural. . . . Well—now you must promise not to laugh at this part of the story, Chris, or I simply shan't be able to tell you—presently he started making the most passionate love to me. At first I was rather angry with him, for sort of mixing business with pleasure; but then, after a bit, I didn't mind so much: he was quite attractive, in a Russian kind of way. . . . And the end of it was, he invited me to have dinner with him; so we went to Horcher's and had one of the most marvellous dinners I've ever had in my life (that's one consolation); only, when

132

the bill came, he said ' Oh, by the way,
darling, could you lend me three
hundred marks until to-morrow ? I've
only got dollar notes on me, and I'll
have to get them changed at the Bank.'
So, of course, I gave them to him: as
bad luck would have it, I had quite a
lot of money on me, that evening. . . .
And then he said: ' Let's have a bottle
of champagne to celebrate your film
contract.' So I agreed, and I suppose
by that time I must have been pretty
tight because when he asked me to
spend the night with him, I said Yes.
We went to one of those little hotels in
the Augsburgerstrasse—I forget its
name, but I can find it again, easily.
. . . It was the most ghastly hole. . . .
Anyhow, I don't remember much more
about what happened that evening. It
was early this morning that I started to

think about things properly, while he was still asleep; and I began to wonder if everything was really quite all right. . . . I hadn't noticed his underclothes before: they gave me a bit of a shock. You'd expect an important film man to wear silk next his skin, wouldn't you? Well, his were the most extraordinary kind of stuff like camel-hair or something; they looked as if they might have belonged to John the Baptist. And then he had a regular Woolworth's tin clip for his tie. It wasn't so much that his things were shabby; but you could see they'd never been any good, even when they were new. . . . I was just making up my mind to get out of bed and take a look inside his pockets, when he woke up and it was too late. So we ordered breakfast. . . . I don't know if he thought I was madly in love

with him by this time and wouldn't
notice, or whether he just couldn't be
bothered to go on pretending, but this
morning he was like a completely different person—just a common little gutter-
snipe. He ate his jam off the blade of
his knife, and of course most of it went
on to the sheets. And he sucked the
insides out of the eggs with a most
terrific squelching noise. I couldn't
help laughing at him, and that made him
quite cross. . . . Then he said: ' I
must have beer!' Well, I said, all
right; ring down to the office and ask
for some. To tell you the truth, I was
beginning to be a bit frightened of him.
He'd started to scowl in the most cave-
mannish way: I felt sure he must be
mad. So I thought I'd humour him as
much as I could. . . . Anyhow, he
seemed to think I'd made quite a good

suggestion, and he picked up the telephone and had a long conversation and got awfully angry, because he said they refused to send beer up to the rooms. I realize now that he must have been holding the hook down all the time and just acting; but he did it most awfully well, and anyhow I was much too scared to notice things much. I thought he'd probably start murdering me because he couldn't get his beer. . . . However, he took it quite quietly. He said he must get dressed and go downstairs and fetch it himself. All right, I said. . . . Well, I waited and waited and he didn't come back. So at last I rang the bell and asked the maid if she'd seen him go out. And she said: ' Oh yes, the gentleman paid the bill and went away about an hour ago. . . . He said you weren't to be disturbed.'

I was so surprised, I just said: ' Oh, right, thanks. . . .' The funny thing was, I'd so absolutely made up my mind by this time that he was a looney that I'd stopped suspecting him of being a swindler. Perhaps that was what he wanted. . . . Anyhow, he wasn't such a looney, after all, because, when I looked in my bag, I found he'd helped himself to all the rest of my money, as well as the change from the three hundred marks I'd lent him the night before. . . . What really annoys me about the whole business is that I bet he thinks I'll be ashamed to go to the police. Well, I'll just show him he's wrong——"

" I say, Sally, what exactly did this young man look like ? "

" He was about your height. Pale. Dark. You could tell he wasn't a born

American; he spoke with a foreign accent——"

"Can you remember if he mentioned a man named Schraube, who lives in Chicago?"

"Let's see . . . Yes, of course he did! He talked about him a lot. . . . But, Chris, how on earth did you know?"

"Well, it's like this. . . . Look here, Sally, I've got a most awful confession to make to you. . . . I don't know if you'll ever forgive me. . . ."

.   .   .

We went to the Alexanderplatz that same afternoon.

The interview was even more embarrassing than I had expected. For myself at any rate. Sally, if she felt uncomfortable, did not show it by so much as the movement of an eyelid. She detailed the facts of the case to the two bespectacled police officials with such brisk bright matter-of-factness that one might have supposed she had come to complain about a strayed lap-dog or an umbrella lost in a bus. The two officials—both obviously fathers of families—were at first inclined to be shocked. They dipped their pens excessively in the violet ink, made nervous inhibited circular movements with their elbows before starting to write, and were very curt and gruff.

"Now about this hotel," said the elder of them sternly: "I suppose you knew, before going there, that it was an hotel of a certain kind?"

"Well, you didn't expect us to go to the Bristol, did you?" Sally's tone was very mild and reasonable: "They wouldn't have let us in there without luggage, anyway."

" Ah, so you had no luggage ? " The younger one pounced upon this fact triumphantly, as of supreme importance. His violet copperplate police-hand began to travel steadily across a ruled sheet of foolscap paper. Deeply inspired by his theme, he paid not the slightest attention to Sally's retort:

" I don't usually pack a suitcase when a man asks me out to dinner."

The elder one caught the point, however, at once:

" So it wasn't till you were at the restaurant that this young man invited you to—er—accompany him to the hotel ? "

" It wasn't till after dinner."

" My dear young lady," the elder one sat back in his chair, very much the sarcastic father, "may I enquire whether it is your usual custom to accept invitations of this kind from perfect strangers ? "

Sally smiled sweetly. She was innocence and candour itself:

" But, you see, Herr Kommissar, he wasn't a perfect stranger. He was my fiancé."

That made both of them sit up with a jerk. The younger one even made a small blot in the middle of his virgin page—the only blot, perhaps, to be found in all the spotless dossiers of the Polizeipräsidium.

" You mean to tell me, Frl Bowles " —but, in spite of his gruffness, there was already a gleam in the elder one's eye—" You mean to tell me that you became engaged to this man when you'd only known him a single afternoon ? "

" Certainly."

" Isn't that, well—rather unusual ? "

" I suppose it is," Sally seriously agreed. " But nowadays, you know, a girl can't afford to keep a man waiting. If he asks her once and she refuses him, he may try somebody else. It's all these surplus women——"

At this, the elder official frankly exploded. Pushing back his chair, he laughed himself quite purple in the face. It was nearly a minute before he could speak at all. The young one was much more decorous; he produced a large handkerchief and pretended to blow his nose. But the nose-blowing developed into a kind of sneeze which became a guffaw; and soon he too had abandoned all attempt to take Sally seriously. The rest of the interview was conducted with comic-opera informality, accompanied by ponderous essays in gallantry. The elder official, particularly, became quite daring: I think they were both sorry that I was present. They wanted her to themselves.

" Now don't you worry, Frl Bowles," they told her, patting her hand at parting, " we'll find him for you, if we have to turn Berlin inside out to do it! "

.   .   .

" Well! " I exclaimed admiringly, as soon as we were out of earshot, " you do know how to handle them, I must say! "

Sally smiled dreamily: she was feeling very pleased with herself: " How do you mean, exactly, darling ? "

" You know as well as I do—getting them to laugh like that: telling them he was your fiancé! It was really inspired!"

But Sally didn't laugh. Instead, she coloured a little, looking down at her feet. A comically guilty, childish expression came over her face:

" You see, Chris, it happened to be quite true——"

" True! "

" Yes, darling." Now, for the first time, Sally was really embarrassed: she began speaking very fast: " I simply couldn't tell you this morning: after everything that's happened, it would have sounded too idiotic for words. . . . He asked me to marry him while we were at the restaurant, and I said Yes. . . . You see, I thought that, being in films, he was probably quite used to quick engagements, like that: after all, in Hollywood, it's quite the usual thing. . . . And, as he was an American, I thought we could get divorced

144

again easily, any time we wanted to.
. . . And it would have been a good
thing for my career—I mean, if he'd
been genuine—wouldn't it ? . . . We
were to have got married to-day, if it
could have been managed. . . . It
seems funny to think of, now——"

"But Sally!" I stood still. I gaped
at her. I had to laugh: "Well really
. . . You know, you're the most extraordinary creature I ever met in my life!"

Sally giggled a little, like a naughty
child which has unintentionally succeeded in amusing the grown-ups:

"I always told you I was a bit mad,
didn't I ? Now perhaps you'll believe
it——"

.   .   .   .

It was more than a week before the
police could give us any news. Then,

one morning, two detectives called to see me. A young man answering to our description had been traced and was under observation. The police knew his address, but wanted me to identify him before making the arrest. Would I come round with them at once to a snack-bar in the Kleiststrasse ? He was to be seen there, about this time, almost every day. I should be able to point him out to them in the crowd and leave again at once, without any fuss or unpleasantness.

I didn't like the idea much, but there was no getting out of it now. The snack-bar, when we arrived, was crowded, for this was the lunch-hour. I caught sight of the young man almost immediately: he was standing at the counter, by the tea-urn, cup in hand. Seen thus, alone and off his guard, he seemed rather pathetic: he looked shabbier and far younger—a mere boy. I very nearly said: " He isn't here." But what would have been the use ? They'd got him, anyway. " Yes, that's him," I told the detectives. " over there." They nodded. I turned and hurried away down the street, feeling guilty and telling myself: I'll never help the police again.

.   .   .

A few days later, Sally came round to tell me the rest of the story: " I had to see him, of course. . . . I felt an awful brute; he looked so wretched. All he said was: ' I thought you were my friend.' I'd have told him he could keep the money, but he'd spent it all, anyway. . . . The police said he really had been to the States, but he isn't

American; he's a Pole. . . . He won't be prosecuted, that's one comfort. The doctor's seen him and he's going to be sent to a home. I hope they treat him decently there. . . ."

" So he was a looney, after all ? "

" I suppose so. A sort of mild one. . . ." Sally smiled. " Not very flattering to me, is it ? Oh, and Chris, do you know how old he was ? You'd never guess! "

" Round about twenty, I should think."

" Sixteen! "

" Oh, rot! "

" Yes, honestly. . . . The case would have to have been tried in the Children's Court! "

We both laughed. " You know, Sally," I said, " what I really like about you is that you're so awfully easy to take in. People who never get taken in are so dreary."

" So you still like me, Chris darling ? "

" Yes, Sally. I still like you."

" I was afraid you'd be angry with me—about the other day."

" I was. Very."

" But you're not, now ? "

" No . . . I don't think so."

" It's no good my trying to apologize, or explain, or anything. . . . I get like that, sometimes. . . . I expect you understand, don't you, Chris ? "

" Yes," I said. " I expect I do."

.   .   .

I have never seen her since. About a fortnight later, just when I was thinking that I ought really to ring her up, I got a post-card from Paris: " Arrived here last night. Will write properly to-morrow. Heaps of love." No letter followed. A month after this, another post-card arrived from Rome, giving no address: "Am writing in a day or two," it said. That was six years ago.

So now I am writing to her.

When you read this, Sally—if you ever do—please accept it as a tribute, the sincerest I can pay, to yourself and to our friendship.

And send me another post-card.